OTHER BOOKS BY RHODA LEVINE
PUBLISHED BY NEW YORK REVIEW BOOKS

Arthur
Illustrated by Everett Aison

He Was There from the Day We Moved In
Illustrated by Edward Gorey

Three Ladies Beside the Sea
Illustrated by Edward Gorey

RHODA LEVINE

illustrated by Karla Kuskin

The New York Review Children's Collection,
New York

Harrison Loved His Umbrella

THIS IS A NEW YORK REVIEW BOOK
PUBLISHED BY THE NEW YORK REVIEW OF BOOKS
435 Hudson Street, New York, NY 10014
www.nyrb.com

A catalog record for this book is available from the Library
of Congress
ISBN 978-159017-991-8
Available as an electronic book; ISBN 978-1-59017-992-5
Cover design by Louise Fili Ltd.
Manufactured in China
1 2 3 4 5 6 7 8 9 10

For my nephews:

Jonathan David and Paul Samuel
who waited patiently for Harrison.

And for:

Madeline, George, Basil, Anne, Danny,
Janet, Martha, Tim, Paul, Bill,
Joe, V. T., Mary, Hazel,
Joseph, Gian Carlo, Ricki, Carole,
Ruth, Bernard, Claudia, Gene,
Cynthia, and Arthur.

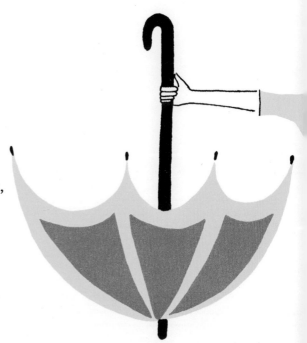

Harrison loved his umbrella.

He liked to hold it in the rain.

He loved

to hold it in the sun.　　　　He found it very helpful in the snow.

But most of all,
he loved to hold it open . . . in the house!

Harrison's umbrella made his
parents very nervous.

They looked upon it
with great consternation.

They felt it was "severely limiting."

Harrison could not open
the toothpaste.

He could not cut with a scissors.

He could not play the piano
with two hands.

In addition,
his father found it difficult to
read to Harrison.

The umbrella was always in the way!

When his mother asked him to close his umbrella,
Harrison wept.

When his father asked him to put his umbrella away,
Harrison howled.

When his brother snatched and tried to hide his umbrella,
Harrison yelled. Then he found it.

"Umbrellas are made for outdoor use!"
his family proclaimed.
But Harrison would not listen.

His umbrella was his best friend, indoors or out.

It was good to talk to.

It was fine to hide behind.

It was good for pretending a pool.

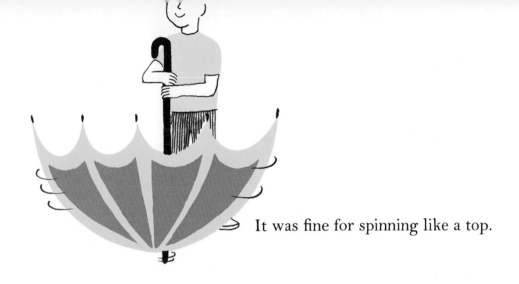

It was fine for spinning like a top.

It made an excellent shield against wild beasts.

Harrison knew that it would be useful
in helping him fly—
should he ever decide to do so.

When he trotted down the street, all his friends admired him.

"I certainly am a somebody," Harrison thought each day.

"A somebody" Harrison certainly was.
He was the only boy on the block to carry an umbrella . . . ALL THE TIME!

Now, one rainy day an unusual thing happened.

Umbrellas were out on the street in full force.

However, on this day, when the rain
stopped, not one child closed his umbrella!
Like Harrison, every child held an open umbrella.

All the children loved their umbrellas
indoors or out.

Now, all the parents on the block became
very nervous.

They found such behavior "severely limiting."

Then, too, when they looked down on their children,
they saw nothing but umbrella tops.
Though this was a colorful sight, they missed
the sight of their children.

"Suppose," they shuddered at the thought, "the
children exchange umbrellas! Suppose we meet a
familiar umbrella on the street and look under
it and find a child we do not even know!!!"

The parents grew more and more nervous.

Many of them started to lose weight!

Some of them cried in the evening.

Soon the parents began to worry
in small groups.

Then they worried in a large group.

"This cannot go on," they cried.

"I have not seen my child for a whole week,"
a rumpled mother wept.

"Down with umbrellas," a weary father muttered.

"Everyone likes to have something to hold on to,"
the parents agreed, "but umbrellas are going too far."

"Down with umbrellas!" they all cried, and they
started to plan. . . .

However, life beneath the umbrellas was perfectly happy.

The children loved their constant companions.

They never had to look up to anyone.

They were always protected.

Going to bed seemed like camping out.
Every child had a tent.

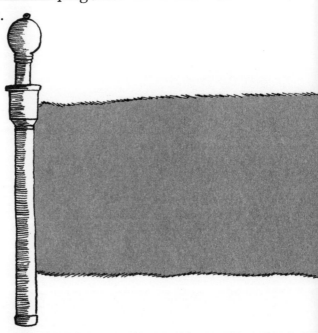

The parents continued to ponder their problem.
Finally, they made what they thought was a
very fine plan.

"We will spend tomorrow in silence," they decided.
"Our children will think we are lost.
They will put aside their umbrellas to
search for us."

Some of the parents smiled for the first time
in a week.

The next day, from dawn to sunset, not one parent
said one word.

But . . . not one child felt that
his parents were lost.
"My mother and father have been quite quiet today,"
each child decided as he watched his parents' feet
walk in the shade of his umbrella.

The next night, the parents discussed their error.

"We must," they concluded, "stand on chairs all day tomorrow. When our children miss our feet, surely they will put their umbrellas aside and search for us."

The following day, all the parents stood on chairs. But the fathers found it hard to leave for work while standing on a chair.
The mothers found they could not cook breakfast from such a height.

Again the children were not worried.
"Our parents are dusting in high, lofty places," all the children thought sympathetically as they stood beneath their umbrellas. "How tired they must be!"

All the parents had to descend.

"Let us," the disgruntled parents decided, "buy each child a new toy to play with. Surely *that* will make them forget their umbrellas!"

The next evening every father came home with a new toy. Each umbrella jumped for joy!

All the children felt they were having another birthday.

They played with their new toys in the shade of their umbrellas. Which they pretended were party hats.

And when dinner came, each child arrived at the table with a toy in one hand . . . and an umbrella in the other!

"We must," the parents concluded, "call a meeting and explain to our children how very much we miss the sight of them."

So they invited their children to a gathering.

The boys and girls were most pleased to accept the invitation.
They would have a chance to see their friends and compare
umbrellas.

The very next day, everyone met at Harrison's house,
since it had the largest living room.
The mothers and fathers stood in a line and faced a
group of dancing umbrellas. The children were skipping
around. They were pretending maypole.

The parents cleared their throats.
"We want to tell you," one father began, "how very
much we miss you . . ."
But he began to sob; he could not go on.

A courageous mother continued, "We feel we have not seen
you in so long a time that . . ."

The children continued to skip as they listened.

Suddenly, a strange sound came from the top
of the stairs.
It was a "whir" and a "whistle" and sometimes
a "clunk."

Everyone looked up.

The children stopped skipping.

The sight they saw made them drop their umbrellas!!!!

There stood Harrison . . .
He was not holding his umbrella open.
He was not holding his umbrella closed.
He was not holding his umbrella at all!

He was, however, holding a spinning, whistling yo-yo.

All the children looked up to Harrison.
How they admired him!

"I certainly am a somebody," Harrison thought.
"A somebody" Harrison certainly was.

He was the only boy on the block to carry a spinning,
whistling yo-yo in his hand . . . ALL THE TIME!

RHODA LEVINE is the author of seven children's books and is an accomplished director and choreographer. In addition to working for major opera houses in the United States and Europe, she has choreographed shows on and off Broadway, and in London's West End. Among the world premieres she has directed are *Der Kaiser von Atlantis* by Viktor Ullmann and *X—The Life and Times of Malcolm X* and *Wakonda's Dream*, both by Anthony Davis. In Cape Town she directed the South African premiere of *Porgy and Bess* in 1996, and she premiered the New York City Opera productions of Janácek's *From the House of the Dead*, Zimmermann's *Die Soldaten*, and Adamo's *Little Women*.

Levine has taught acting and improvisation at the Yale School of Drama, the Curtis Institute of Music, and Northwestern University, and is currently on the faculty of the Manhattan School of Music and the Mannes College of Music. She lives in New York, where she is the artistic director of the city's only improvisational opera company, Play It by Ear.

KARLA KUSKIN (1932–2009) was born in Manhattan and grew up in the Greenwich Village neighborhood of the city. She attended Antioch College before transferring to Yale, where she studied with Josef Albers and earned a bachelor of fine arts in graphic design in 1955. With the publication of her first book, *Roar and More* (1956), she embarked on a lifelong career as a writer and illustrator, going on to produce more than fifty books. Among the many artists and authors she worked with were Paula Fox, Peter Viertel, and Marc Simont, who provided the illustrations to *The Philharmonic Gets Dressed*, a finalist for the 1983 National Book Award for children's picture book.

TITLES IN THE NEW YORK REVIEW
CHILDREN'S COLLECTION

ESTHER AVERILL
Captains of the City Streets
The Hotel Cat
Jenny and the Cat Club
Jenny Goes to Sea
Jenny's Birthday Book
Jenny's Moonlight Adventure
The School for Cats

JAMES CLOYD BOWMAN
Pecos Bill: The Greatest Cowboy
 of All Time

PALMER BROWN
Beyond the Pawpaw Trees
Cheerful
Hickory
The Silver Nutmeg
Something for Christmas

SHEILA BURNFORD
Bel Ria: Dog of War

MARY CHASE
Loretta Mason Potts

CARLO COLLODI and FULVIO TESTA
Pinocchio

INGRI and EDGAR PARIN D'AULAIRE
D'Aulaires' Book of Animals
D'Aulaires' Book of Norse Myths
D'Aulaires' Book of Trolls
Foxie: The Singing Dog
The Terrible Troll-Bird
Too Big
The Two Cars

EILÍS DILLON
The Island of Horses
The Lost Island

ELEANOR FARJEON
The Little Bookroom

PENELOPE FARMER
Charlotte Sometimes

PAUL GALLICO
The Abandoned

LEON GARFIELD
The Complete Bostock and Harris
Leon Garfield's Shakespeare Stories
Smith: The Story of a Pickpocket

RUMER GODDEN
An Episode of Sparrows
The Mousewife

MARIA GRIPE and HARALD GRIPE
The Glassblower's Children

LUCRETIA P. HALE
The Peterkin Papers

RUSSELL and LILLIAN HOBAN
The Sorely Trying Day

RUTH KRAUSS and MARC SIMONT
The Backward Day

DOROTHY KUNHARDT
Junket Is Nice
Now Open the Box

MUNRO LEAF and ROBERT LAWSON
Wee Gillis

RHODA LEVINE and EVERETT AISON
Arthur

RHODA LEVINE and EDWARD GOREY
He Was There from the Day We Moved In
Three Ladies Beside the Sea

BETTY JEAN LIFTON
and EIKOH HOSOE
Taka-chan and I

ASTRID LINDGREN
Mio, My Son
Seacrow Island

NORMAN LINDSAY
The Magic Pudding

ERIC LINKLATER
The Wind on the Moon

J. P. MARTIN
Uncle
Uncle Cleans Up

JOHN MASEFIELD
The Box of Delights
The Midnight Folk

WILLIAM McCLEERY
and WARREN CHAPPELL
Wolf Story

JEAN MERRILL and RONNI SOLBERT
The Elephant Who Liked to Smash
  Small Cars
The Pushcart War

E. NESBIT
The House of Arden

ALFRED OLLIVANT's
Bob, Son of Battle: The Last Gray
  Dog of Kenmuir
A New Version by LYDIA DAVIS

DANIEL PINKWATER
Lizard Music

OTFRIED PREUSSLER
Krabat & the Sorcerer's Mill
The Little Water Sprite
The Little Witch

VLADIMIR RADUNSKY
and CHRIS RASCHKA
Alphabetabum

ALASTAIR REID and BOB GILL
Supposing…

ALASTAIR REID and BEN SHAHN
Ounce Dice Trice

BARBARA SLEIGH
Carbonel and Calidor
Carbonel: The King of the Cats
The Kingdom of Carbonel

E. C. SPYKMAN
Terrible, Horrible Edie

FRANK TASHLIN
The Bear That Wasn't

VAL TEAL and ROBERT LAWSON
The Little Woman Wanted Noise

JAMES THURBER
The 13 Clocks
The Wonderful O

ALISON UTTLEY
A Traveller in Time

T. H. WHITE
Mistress Masham's Repose

MARJORIE WINSLOW
and ERIK BLEGVAD
Mud Pies and Other Recipes

REINER ZIMNIK
The Bear and the People